MY MIDDOS WORLD

My Middos World was first published in Hebrew in 1993 and immediately became a best seller. Tens of thousands of copies were sold, benefiting hundreds of educators and parents.

What makes this series so outstanding? Besides being so beautiful in every aspect – impressive pictures, special laminated paper, a large size format – the contents of the books are very special indeed. The stories are written in a simple manner, yet they convey a deep Jewish message. They portray the beauty of good middos from a Torah outlook and teach us to perform Mitzvos happily and wholeheartedly.

The books elicit the positive potential in every child and help him see the beauty in himself and in the Torah world surrounding him.

We hope that *My Middos World* will bring great enjoyment and benefit to young Jewish children throughout the world.

Published by:
Beckerman Publishers
19 Lubavitch St, Ramat Shlomo,
Jerusalem, 97520
Tel: (02)-5863796 Fax: (02)-5862598
Email:beckermn@bezeqint.net

Distributed by:
Israel Book Shop
501 Prospect St, Lakewood, NJ, 08701
Tel: (732)-901-3009
Fax: (732)-901-4012
Email: isrbkshp@aol.com

בס"ד

Menuchah Beckerman

AVI AND CHAVI VISIT THE FARM

Illustrated by Tirza Peleg

Avi and Chavi live in Eretz Yisroel. One beautiful summer day, they waited excitedly for the van that was going to take them to the farm. They were going to be guests of Uncle Chaim and Aunt Rivka for two whole weeks.

Their clothes were packed neatly in a red suitcase. Avi held the suitcase tightly. They looked out the window and waited impatiently. 'When will the van come? How long will they have to wait?'

"Here it is!" shouted Avi, when he saw the yellow van pull up in front of their house. The two children flew down the steps. Ephraim, the driver, opened the van's big door. Avi and Chavi jumped inside.

"Goodbye! Goodbye!" They called to Mommy, blowing her kisses. Efraim closed the door, and off they went.

"Bye, Yehuda. We're going to the farm!" they shouted through the window to their friend. He waved to them with both hands.

"Goodbye, Mrs. Rosen! See you in two weeks! We're going to visit our uncle on the farm!" they announced at the top of their lungs.

"Have a good, safe trip!" the neighbor replied.

On and on the van drove. They came to streets they did not recognize. The van kept speeding along. Now they were on the main road - a big, wide highway. Many cars and buses were on the highway.

"Look at that double-decker bus!" Chavi pointed out.

"And at that low-flying airplane!" Avi shouted.

The van traveled very fast. There were just hills and mountains, trees and fields on the both sides of the highway.

"It's time to say Tefillas Haderech", said Ephraim, and he recited the Tefilla out loud. Avi and Chavi repeated it after him, word for word. They knew that the Tefilla kept them safe from accidents and other dangers.

Ephraim was an excellent driver, and Avi and Chavi sang him a special song:

"Ephraim our driver is always tops! He drives and drives and never stops! He can travel many miles, and always does it with big smiles!"

Ephraim kept driving. He passed many beautiful and interesting places, but his two passengers, Avi and Chavi, didn't see them. They had dozed off and were sleeping soundly!

"Here we are!" Ephraim announced about an hour later, as he parked the van at the entrance to the farm. Avi and Chavi woke up, and who was waiting for them when they opened their eyes? Uncle Chaim! Avi grabbed the suitcase, and the two children jumped out of the van right into their uncle's open arms.

Uncle Chaim was big and strong. He could pick them up and hold both of them at the same time. They loved to visit their favorite uncle! They missed him, because they hadn't seen him since Pesach when he had come visit them.

On the Seder night, Avi stole the Afikoman from Uncle Chaim. He and Chavi decided to ask for a trip to the farm as their Afikoman present.

Uncle Chaim was very happy when he heard their request, and he promised to invite them over to his house during their summer vacation.

A long time had passed since Pesach. Now, finally, summer arrived, and Uncle Chaim kept his promise.

"Thank you very much, Mr. Ephraim. You are a great driver!" the children shouted as the van pulled out.

"See you, children! I will be back to bring you home!" Ephraim replied.

He waved goodbye - and off he drove.

Uncle Chaim picked up the children and put them on a wagon that was hitched to two horses - one was big and one was small.

"What an adorable pony!" said Chavi. "I feel like giving it a hug."

"How does the horse know where to go?" asked Avi.

"It has straps around its mouth, and reins go through those straps. I use those reins in order to 'talk' to it. When I pull to the right, it turns right, and when I pull to the left, it knows that it should turn left. If I pull both of them together, it gallops straight ahead," explained Uncle Chaim, and he called, "Giddyap! Giddyap!"

"You have smart horses!" marveled the children.

Although the wagon was much slower than the van, it was much more fun. It bounced up and down, and it gave them a good view of everything around them.

"Let me hold the reins," Avi begged. Uncle Chaim agreed, and Avi felt very brave and strong. Chavi admired his courage.

"Giddyap! Giddyap!" Avi shouted out loud. He was so excited that he pulled the reins very hard. The horses jumped up on their hind legs and the children were bounced off their seats.

"Help!" Chavi screamed. She was frightened. Uncle Chaim took over the reins quickly. "It's not easy to be a wagon driver!" he smiled.

Uncle Chaim drove the wagon into the farm.
"Whoa!" he shouted, and the horses stopped in front of his house.

Their uncle's house was just one story high, like the rest of the houses on the farm. There were large spaces between the houses, and each house, had a huge lawn.

Aunt Rivka hugged them tight. "Here are our special guests. I've been looking forward to your visit very much!" she said.

Then she served them a drink - milk! Aunt Rivka said that only her milk was natural. "The milk you drink at home was processed and it lost its real flavor! Here, on the farm, the milk is pure and real." Avi and Chavi liked the farm milk. It had a special taste, like sweet cream. They each drank a big, full cup, without even adding chocolate flavor.

As soon as they finished drinking, they ran outside. The garden was very pretty. To the right, there were neat vegetable patches.

The children bent down and looked closely at them. "What's growing over here? All I see are leaves!" Chavi remarked.

"Look under the leaves, and maybe you'll see something peeking out!" suggested their uncle. The two children crouched closely to the ground and looked.

"Here, under this leaf, I see something purple and tiny. What is it?" asked Chavi.

"Go ahead, pick it," said Uncle Chaim. "Wow...! Look...! I picked a cute little radish!" Chavi was thrilled.

"Now I understand why the brocho for radishes is Borei pri ha'adomo!" cried Avi. "It's because we take it right out of the adomo - the ground!"

"Very good. You are a smart boy," Uncle Chaim praised him. "The brocho for all plants that grow in the ground is Borei pri ha'adomo."

"But I see tomatoes in the next patch. They are not growing in the ground. They are above the ground. Why do we say Borei pri ha'adomo on them too? Why don't we say Borei pri ha'etz?" asked Chavi.

"You are very smart, and you are asking excellent questions. Listen, and I'll explain why. A tree is planted once, and that's it! The tree trunk and branches last for many years. They do not need to be planted again. Each year, fresh fruit grows on the tree. We say Borei pri ha'etz on fruit because it grows on trees.

"Vegetables are different. They don't have tree trunks or branches that remain from year to year. Every year, we plant vegetables over again.

"Look - after we picked the radishes, nothing was left in the ground. There were no trees and no branches. Next year, we will plant them again. That's why we say Borei pri ha'adomo before we eat them. We do the same for tomatoes. Every year, we plant them again."

The children looked at the rest of the vegetable patch. The carrots also played "hide and seek", just like the radishes. They hid inside the ground, under the leaves. The red, shiny tomatoes which they had picked made their mouths water. The peppers looked a bit like flowers, as they stood tall on their stems.

Chavi gathered all the vegetables into her skirt, and they went back into the house.

"I am going to taste one of these adorable little radishes!" Chavi announced. She was about to make a brocho and bite into it, when Uncle Chaim shouted, "Oh, no! Don't eat them!"

Chavi was startled, "Why can't we eat the radishes? What's wrong with them?"

"The radish you picked is tevel! We didn't take ma'aser from it yet," answered Uncle Chaim.

"But what is tevel, and how do you take ma'aser? Chavi asked.

Uncle Chaim explained, "From whatever grows in Eretz Yisroel, we must separate a small part, and this is called 'trumos and ma'asros'. Until we do, we are not allowed to eat those fruits and vegetables. They are called 'tevel', and they are like food that isn't kosher

"Eretz Yisroel is the only land that has kedusha, that is why we take ma'aser from whatever grows here. We farmers are lucky to be able to keep the special Mitzvos of Eretz Yisroel."

"Boruch Hashem you stopped me in

time!" cried Chavi.

Uncle Chaim cut off a little piece of each type of vegetable, put it aside, and said the brocho out loud, "Boruch atoh... l'hafrish terumos uma'asros."

Then he said a long paragraph that the children did not understand. They heard him say something about terumos and ma'asros, and some other big words. Then he put the pieces that he had set aside into a little plastic bag, made a knot, and dropped it into a garbage can.

"That's all! Now the vegetables are not tevel anymore - they are ready for us to eat!" announced Uncle Chaim.

Aunt Rivka washed the rest of the vegetables and cut them into big pieces. She put them on plates, together with some of her special cheese.

Avi and Chavi made a loud brocho - Borei pri ha'adomo - and bit into the radishes. "Mmmm... they taste great! They're delicious!" they said.

Aunt Rivka did not buy cheese in a store, she prepared it by herself. When milk would turn sour, she would pour it into a pitcher, add a little bit of plain yogurt and warm it up. The milk would curdle and turn into cheese with water around it. She would then pour it into a cloth bag that hung over the milchig sink. The water would drip into the sink and only good fresh cheese would remain in the bag. Avi and Chavi enjoyed it to the last drop. "Too bad we don't have such delicious, fresh food in our house." sighed Chavi.

"Don't worry, you can grow vegetables, too!" Aunt Rivka assured her. "When it's time for you to go, Uncle Chaim will give you seeds and teach you how to grow vegetables in your own back yard."

"And where will we get such good, homemade cheese?" asked Chavi.

"That's no problem at all. You can also make your own cheese from the milk that you buy in the store! Your mommy knows exactly how to make it," explained Aunt Rivka.

"What a great idea! We'll take the farm with us when we go home!" said the children happily, clapping their hands.

Long last!!!
Those 8 adorable, beautiful, educational, *'My Little World'* books have been reprinted!!!

'MY LITTLE WORLD' books have captured the hearts of tens of thousands of Jewish children around the world since 1986. What makes these books so popular is the detailed attention that was given to every aspect of their production.

The size is small and personal, perfect for those small hands. **The language** is simple to understand, no 'big' words to explain, with very attractive **full color illustrations.** The characters are taken from every child's life. The plot comes right out of the childrens' *little world*, from their trials and tribulations, disappointments and achievements. **The moral message** is interwoven in the plot so that the child can identify and accept it as if it was a personal experience. The books were written by Menuchah Beckerman.